Dr. Carbles Is Losing His Marbles!

Dr. Carbles Is Losing His Marbles!

Dan Gutman

Pictures by
Jim Paillot

SCHOLASTIC INC.

ISBN 978-0-545-92536-5

Text copyright © 2007 by Dan Gutman. Illustrations copyright © 2007 by Jim Paillot. All rights reserved. Published by Scholastic Inc., 557 Broadway, New York, NY 10012, by arrangement with HarperCollins Children's Books, a division of HarperCollins Publishers. SCHOLASTIC and associated logos are trademarks and/or registered trademarks of Scholastic Inc.

12 11 10 9 8 7 6 5 4   17 18 19 20/0

Printed in the U.S.A.   40

First Scholastic printing, October 2015

Typography by Joel Tippie

To Emma

To Emma

Contents

Squanto and Pocahontas

My name is A.J. and I hate school.

Do you know what the only good part of school is? The *end* of it, at three o'clock, when we get to go home!

But at the end of school this one day in November, we weren't allowed to go home at three. The school secretary, Mrs. Patty, made an announcement that everybody had to go to the all-purpose room. (That's a room we use for all purposes, so it has the perfect name.)

Bummer in the summer!

So we were sitting there, bored out of our minds, when suddenly two American Indians came running down the aisle! They were wearing feathers and head-dresses. They jumped onto the stage, whooping and hollering.

But they couldn't fool us. We knew exactly who they were.

"It's Mrs. Roopy!" yelled my friend Michael, who never ties his shoes. Mrs. Roopy is our librarian.

"And Mr. Klutz!" yelled my friend Ryan, who will eat anything, even stuff that isn't food. Mr. Klutz is our principal, and he has no hair.

"Klutz?" said Mr. Klutz. "Never heard of him. I am Squanto, a Patuxet Indian who helped the Pilgrims survive their first years in America."

"And I am Pocahontas," said Mrs. Roopy. "I helped the English colonists when they arrived in Virginia in 1607."

Mrs. Roopy always dresses up like somebody else. She never admits she's the librarian.

Mrs. Roopy is loopy.

"Thanksgiving is coming up," said Mr.

Klutz. "To celebrate, we want to introduce you to a friend of ours."

They went behind the curtain, and
you'll never believe in a million hundred
years who they brought out onstage with
them.

I'm not going to tell you.

Okay, okay, I'll tell you. But you have
to read the next chapter. So nah-nah-nah
boo-boo on you.

Turkeys Are Weird

It was a turkey! They brought a turkey right out onstage!

Now, I've seen plenty of dead turkeys in sandwiches, but I've never seen a live one before. This turkey was dressed like a Pilgrim, with a little bonnet and dress. It was hilarious. All the kids went nuts.

"Gobble, gobble," said the turkey.

"Where do you think Mr. Klutz got a turkey?" asked Neil Crouch, who we call Neil the nude kid even though he wears clothes.

"Maybe he rented it," said Michael. "You can rent anything. There's

probably a place called Rent-a-Turkey."

"For my birthday party, my parents rented a lady dressed like a clown," said Ryan. "If you can rent a lady dressed like a clown, then you can probably rent a turkey dressed like a lady."

"For *my* birthday party, my parents rented a pony," said this annoying girl with curly brown hair named Andrea Young. "We all got pony rides."

Why can't a pony fall on her head?

Mr. Klutz had his arms wrapped around the turkey so she couldn't escape. She didn't look very happy.

"This is our friend Gobbles," said Mrs. Roopy. "She's going to help us get into the spirit of Thanksgiving."

Everybody yelled "HELLO" to Gobbles.

"Gobble, gobble," said Gobbles, flapping her wings. Mr. Klutz was having a hard time holding on to her.

"Isn't Gobbles cute?" asked Andrea.

"No," I said.

What is her problem? Turkeys aren't *cute*. Penguins are cute. Turkeys are ugly. If they were cute, we wouldn't eat them. You don't see anybody eating penguins, do you? Besides, if Andrea thinks something is cute, then I don't.

"Gobble, gobble," said Gobbles again. She was really flapping her wings hard now.

Turkeys are weird. They can't fly. What's

the point of being a bird if you can't fly? That would be like being a fish that can't swim. Gobbles was probably upset because Thanksgiving was coming. If I was a turkey, I would hate Thanksgiving, too.

"I'll make a deal with you," said Mr. Klutz, who is always making deals with us. "If each class creates a beautiful Thanksgiving display, I will get married to Gobbles."

Wow! It would be cool to see Mr. Klutz marry a turkey. This was going to be even better than the time he kissed a pig on the lips.

Everybody was going crazy, cheering and stamping their feet. Gobbles didn't seem to like all that noise. She started

gobbling really loud. Then she freaked
out and broke away from Mr. Klutz!

Gobbles went running off the stage! She
jumped into the front row, where
the first graders sit! The
first graders freaked out,

shrieking and crying and running away! Then *everybody* started freaking out!

"Run for your lives!" shouted Neil the nude kid. "There's a wild turkey on the loose!"

All the kids were screaming and running and crashing into each other. You should have been there!

And you'll never believe who came into the all-purpose room at that very moment.

It was Dr. Carbles, the president of the Board of Education!

I always thought Mr. Klutz was important, like he was the king of the school. But if Mr. Klutz is like the king of the school, then Dr. Carbles is like the king of the *world*. He probably sits on a throne and has servants fan him with big feathers. I saw that in a movie once.

"KLUTZ!" he hollered. "What's the meaning of this? Why is it that every time I come to this school, you're in some weird costume and the students are running around like lunatics?"

"It's just a little discipline problem, sir," Mr. Klutz said as he chased Gobbles around. "I'm going to put Gobbles in

detention."

"Don't you have any sense, Klutz?" shouted Dr. Carbles. "We have enough discipline problems with the children. Why would you bring a turkey to school?"

"To marry it," somebody said.

That's when Gobbles went berserk. She crashed into Dr. Carbles and knocked him down!

"That's it, Klutz!" Dr. Carbles yelled. "You're FIRED!"

3

Meet the New Boss

What?! Mr. Klutz was *fired*? It couldn't be true! We were all shocked.

I thought it was one of those times when something really horrible happens and then it turns out just to be a dream. I saw that in a movie once.

But the next morning while we were putting our backpacks away, everybody was talking about what happened.

"Dr. Carbles can't fire Mr. Klutz!" said Michael.

"Well, he *did*," said Ryan.

"But Mr. Klutz is the best principal in the world!" said Neil the nude kid.

Neil was right. Everybody loved Mr. Klutz. I was sad. Some kids were crying. Teachers were hugging each other in the hallway and dabbing their eyes with tissues. It was like Mr. Klutz had died.

After we pledged the allegiance, our teacher, Miss Daisy, said we should remember the good times we had with Mr. Klutz.

"Remember when he got his foot caught at the top of the flagpole and was hanging upside down?" said Ryan.

"Remember when he dressed like Santa in the holiday pageant, and he was hanging upside down from his sleigh?" said Michael.

"Once I got called to his office, and he was hanging upside down

from the ceiling," I told everybody.

"Mr. Klutz sure hangs upside down a lot," said Emily, who is a big crybaby.

It was hard to concentrate on reading and math that morning. We were all thinking about the good old days with Mr. Klutz. When it was time to go to the vomitorium for lunch, we were still talking about him.

"They'll have to get us a new principal," said Andrea, who was sitting with her annoying girl friends at the next table.

"Who do you think it will be?" asked Ryan.

"I hope he's nice," said Emily, who always hopes everybody will be nice.

"How do you know it will be a *he*?" said

17

Andrea. "Maybe the principal will be a lady."

"Maybe one of the teachers will become principal," Michael said. "Like Mr. Docker or Ms. Hannah."

"Being principal is an important job," said Neil the nude kid. "There's lots to do, like yell at kids and boss around teachers."

"And dress up in weird costumes and marry turkeys," I added.

"It will be hard to find someone who can fill Mr. Klutz's shoes," said Andrea.

"Who cares about filling his shoes?" I said. "We just need a new principal. What would they fill his shoes with anyway?"

"It's just an expression, dumbhead,"

Andrea said.

"So is your face," I told her.

We didn't have to wait long to find out who the new principal would be. At the end of the day, we had to go to the all-purpose room again. Once everybody was seated, a lady got up onstage. She told us her name was Mrs. Haney and she was the superintendent of all the schools in the county.

Wow! And we thought Dr. Carbles was important. If Dr. Carbles is like the king of the world, then Mrs. Haney is like the queen of the *universe*.

"I bet she can fly and see through walls," I whispered to Michael. "That's

why she's Super Intendent."

Mrs. Haney said she knew we were sad about Mr. Klutz and told us not to worry. Nothing would change now that he was gone.

"I'd like to introduce you to your *new* principal," she announced.

And you'll never believe in a million

hundred years who walked out on the stage.

I'm not going to tell you.

Okay, okay, I'll tell you. And you don't even have to read the next chapter.

It was Dr. Carbles!

Dr. Carbles Is a Meanie

DR. CARBLES?!!?!?!?!?!?!?!?!?!?!?!?!?!?!?!?!?!?!

I always thought you had to go to principal school to be a principal. But I guess any dumbhead can be a principal.

Dr. Carbles wasn't wearing his usual jacket and tie. He was wearing an army uniform, with black boots and a whistle around his neck. In one hand he was holding a bullhorn. In the other he had a whip.

He didn't say anything at first. He just walked down the aisle, looking us over. Nobody made a move. Nobody made a sound. It was so quiet, you could hear a pin drop.*

We were all afraid of Dr. Carbles. He had a scowl on his face. Even Miss Daisy looked scared.

Finally Dr. Carbles put the bullhorn to his mouth.

---

*I mean one of those skinny little pins you use to sew stuff, not a bowling pin. Bowling pins actually make a *lot* of noise when they drop. But you could have heard one of those drop, too, it was so quiet.

"ATTEN–TION!" Dr. Carbles hollered, and we all straightened up in our seats. "This school is pathetic! You are unruly! You are undisciplined! You are totally disrespectful! I won't stand for it!"

He was really mad!

"You don't go to school to have *fun*!" he shouted. "You go to school to *learn*, so you can get into college and have a productive life."

"But I'm only in first grade!" said one of the first graders. Then she started to cry.

"Silence!" shouted Dr. Carbles. He cracked his whip, and everybody jumped. "There are going to be some changes around here. Mr. Klutz was too easy on you. There will be no more turkeys and silly costumes and contests. From now on we will focus on the four Rs: reading, writing, arithmetic, and rules.** We're going to

***

**That didn't make any sense at all, because only two of those words started with R.

turn you students into lean, mean learning machines. And if you don't like the way I do things, well, maybe you'd like to spend a little time in the dungeon on the third floor. Do I make myself clear?"

"Yes, Dr. Carbles," everybody mumbled.

"Children behave better when they're wearing uniforms," Dr. Carbles told us. "So from now on, you will wear the official uniform of Ella Mentry School."

The PTA moms went up and down the rows, passing out a bag to each of us.

"That's all for now," Dr. Carbles said. "Any questions?"

"Can I go to the bathroom?" somebody asked.

"No!" Dr. Carbles yelled. "Weak bladders lead to weak minds. Do you think George Washington went to the bathroom when he was crossing the Delaware?"

"They had bathrooms on the Delaware?" asked Ryan.

"Will we still have recess?" somebody else asked.

"No!" Dr. Carbles yelled. "Recess is for wimps."

"Will we still be allowed to play in the playground after school?" Michael asked.

"NO!" Dr. Carbles yelled. "You're going to MARCH in the playground after school."

Sure enough, when the three-o'clock

bell rang, Dr. Carbles led us out onto the
playground. We had to form a line, with
the fifth graders at the front and the
kindergarten trolls at the back.

"Left! Right! Left! Right!" Dr. Carbles
yelled as we marched. "Stop lagging

behind, kindergarteners!"

Dr. Carbles had us march around the playground a million hundred times. I thought I was gonna die.

Being Frank

The next morning everybody was wearing the official school uniform. The boys had on light blue shirts, blue pants, and blue ties. The girls had on blue skirts with stripes on them.

I looked like a dork. But *everybody* looked like a dork, so I didn't feel so bad.

We were putting our backpacks away when Mrs. Patty's voice came over the loudspeaker.

"A.J., please report to Dr. Carbles's office."

"Ooooooooooooooh!" everybody went.

"A.J. is absent today," I lied.

"Get down here, A.J.," said Mrs. Patty.

"Oooooooooooooooh!"

"You're in trouble, Arlo," said Andrea.

"Dr. Carbles is going to send you to jail."

What did I do? I mean, I know I did a lot of bad stuff. But not recently. It had been *weeks* since I wrote in the boys' bathroom that Andrea was a poopy head. Maybe Dr. Carbles was going to torture me in the dungeon on the third floor. Who knew what he might do to me?

I decided to take my time getting to Dr. Carbles's office. So I started counting the tiles in the hallway.

Did you know that there are 4,324 tiles between Miss Daisy's class and Dr. Carbles's office? I didn't.

As I was walking down the hall, a thought popped into my head. Maybe Dr.

Carbles was going to give me a candy bar! One time I got in trouble and had to go to Mr. Klutz's office. I thought he was going to punish me, but he gave me a candy bar instead. It was the greatest day of my life.

Finally I opened the door to Dr. Carbles's office. It looked a lot different from when Mr. Klutz was principal. The cool snowboarding poster was gone. The Foosball table and the punching bag were gone. Do you know what Dr. Carbles had all over his office instead?

Fish!

There was a fish tank on the windowsill. There was a fishing pole in the

corner. Dr. Carbles even had a picture of himself with a giant fish he'd caught. There was even a real fish that was mounted on the wall.

People who like fish that much are weird.

"What took you so long?" Dr. Carbles asked.

I didn't know what to say. I didn't know what to do. I had to think fast.

"I broke my leg," I lied.

"Shake it off!" Dr. Carbles ordered. "Do you think a broken leg would have stopped George Washington when he was crossing the Delaware?"

"I guess not," I said.

"A.J.," he said more softly, "do you know why I called you in here?"

"Because I wrote in the boys' bathroom that Andrea was a poopy head?"

"What?" yelled Dr. Carbles. "You wrote in the boys' bathroom that Andrea was a poopy head?"

"Uh, no," I said quickly. "What gave you that idea?" It was weird just hearing a principal say "poopy head."

"A.J., can I be Frank?" Dr. Carbles asked.

"I don't care what you call yourself," I told him.

"I asked you to come here because I need to talk with an average student," he said. "Do you know why I fired Mr. Klutz?"

"Because he wanted to marry a turkey?" I guessed.

"No, I fired Mr. Klutz because he's incompetent."

"He wears diapers?" I asked.

"Not incontinent!" Dr. Carbles yelled. "Incompetent! It means he didn't do a good job."

"But we all love Mr. Klutz," I said.

"A.J., I'm going to be Frank," said Dr. Carbles.

"Okay, Frank. I'll be A.J."

"I've never been a principal before," he admitted. "This is all new to me. I need to know what it is about Mr. Klutz that you kids love so much."

"I guess it's because he's silly," I said. "Mr. Klutz is like a big kid."

"A.J., let me be Frank," said Dr. Carbles.

"I already said you could be Frank," I told him.

"It's just not in my nature to be silly," Dr. Carbles said. "When I see the shenanigans at your school, I'm disgusted."

I didn't know what "shenanigans" were, but I didn't tell him that. I bet Andrea knows. She read the whole encyclopedia so she could show off how smart she is. What's up with that?

"If you don't like our shenanigans, maybe we could get some new shenanigans," I suggested.

"A.J., let's be Frank," Dr. Carbles said.

I slapped my forehead.

"You mean *both* of us?" I asked. "Won't that be confusing?"

"Enough! I know what you're trying to do, young man. You're trying to mess with my mind. Well, it won't work. Get out of my office!"

"Okay, Frank," I said.

I got up to leave but stopped at the door.

"Can I have a candy bar, Frank?" I asked.

"No! And stop calling me Frank!"

Sheesh, what a sourpuss! *He's* the one who said to call him Frank.

If you ask me, Dr. Carbles needs to take a chill pill.

Dr. Carbles Is Watching You

When I got back to class, everybody was working on our Thanksgiving display. Miss Daisy said we should still make one even if Mr. Klutz wasn't our principal anymore.

We spent all morning learning about Thanksgiving. The first one was in 1621, and it went on for three days. That's a long meal! Back then the Pilgrims only had knives and spoons. They didn't have any forks. Maybe if they had forks, it wouldn't have taken them three days to eat dinner.

Did you know that at the first Thanksgiving the Pilgrims didn't just eat turkey? They also ate ducks, geese, and swans. Ugh, disgusting!

It was fun making the display, but nobody was happy. We all knew that in the afternoon there would be more marching, more yelling, and more rules.

When we got to the vomitorium for lunch, all the posters about exercising and the Food Pyramid were gone. There

were new posters that said NO TALKING!, BEHAVE, OR ELSE!, and SHUT UP AND EAT! There was even a video camera mounted on the wall with a sign under it that said DR. CARBLES IS WATCHING YOU. We had to whisper, because none of us wanted to get sent to Dr. Carbles's office.

"I heard Dr. Carbles is going to put up guard towers and barbed wire around the school so we can't escape," Ryan whispered.

"We may have to dig a tunnel to get out," I whispered to the guys. "I saw that in a movie once."

"I heard that he punishes kids by putting them into solitary confinement," whispered Michael.

"They're forced to play solitaire?" I whispered back.

"Solitary confinement isn't the same as solitaire, dumbhead," whispered Andrea, who was sitting at the next table.

"Is too," I whispered.

We whispered back and forth like that for a while until I had to whisper "So is your face" to Andrea. But I knew I was right, because my mom plays that game solitary confinement on her computer.

"I miss Mr. Klutz," whispered Emily.

"I'm worried about him," whispered Andrea. "My mother is a psychologist, and she said that people who lose their jobs can get depressed."

"We've got to do something!" Emily whispered.

"We should go over to his house and cheer him up," Michael whispered.

"How would we find out where he

lives?" whispered Neil the nude kid.

"My mother is vice president of the PTA," Andrea whispered. "She knows everything."

Suddenly Dr. Carbles burst into the vomitorium with his bullhorn.

"Knock it off!" he yelled. "It's time for the lunchtime march! Let's go!"

We all jumped up and got into line outside the door.

"Hop to it!" Dr. Carbles hollered. "Left! Right! March! Move it, kindergarteners! You're slow and weak! I want each of you to give me twenty push-ups!"

Dr. Carbles is losing his marbles!

The Truth About Dr. Carbles

Well, I had to admit that Andrea came through for us. Her mother got Mr. Klutz's address, and on Saturday we all piled into her van to go visit him.

The van was big enough to hold Andrea, Emily, me, Ryan, Michael, and Neil the nude kid. Andrea's mom needs a big van because she is always taking

Andrea and her annoying girly friends to dance lessons and cooking lessons and piano lessons and every other kind of lessons they have. If they gave lessons on how to clip your toenails, Andrea would take them so she could get better at it.

I was really surprised when we got to Mr. Klutz's address. I thought he would live in a castle, since he was king of the school. But it was just a regular old house. Ryan rang the doorbell, and a lady came out.

"May I help you?" she asked. "I'm Karla Klutz."

Wow! Mr. Klutz never told us he had a wife! I wonder if she knew her husband was going to marry a turkey.

"Is Mr. Klutz home?" Andrea's mom asked.

"Yes, please come inside."

She led us into the living room. And you'll never believe in a million hundred years what we saw in there.

It was a half-pipe!

Mr. Klutz had a giant half-pipe right in the middle of his living room! Not only that, but he was skateboarding on it! He

did a frontside 180 ollie and a handstand fingerflip and a coconut wheelie. He was really good!

"*Wooooo-hooooooooooooo!*" yelled Mr. Klutz. "Watch this!"

He tried to do an inverted nosegrab, but he messed up, and it turned into a spectacular faceplant.***

"Are you okay?" we all asked as we ran over to help him.

"Of course!" he said. "To what do I owe the pleasure of your company?" (That's grown-up talk for "What are you doing here?")

"We were afraid you'd be depressed,"

***That means he crashed, in case you don't speak Skateboard.

Andrea told him, "so we came to cheer you up."

"Me? Depressed?" said Mr. Klutz. "I've never been happier! I don't have to write reports anymore or deal with crazy teachers, pushy parents, or obnoxious kids. Finally, I have time to chase my dream."

"What's your dream?" Neil the nude kid asked.

"To become a championship skateboarder," Mr. Klutz said.

"Cool!" said all the boys.

"But you're a great principal!" said Andrea, who never misses the chance to brownnose a grown-up. "We need you back at school."

"Dr. Carbles is driving us crazy," Michael said.

"Yes, Milton can be a bit hard to deal with," said Mr. Klutz.

"Milton?!" I said. "He told me his name was Frank!"

"I don't know about that," said Mr. Klutz, "but do you know why he fired me?"

"Because you wear diapers?" I asked.

"No," Mr. Klutz said. "Milton and I grew up together. He was my rival when we were teenagers. We were the two best skaters on the local skateboarding team. Then one day we got into an argument and I called him Walrus Face. From then on, *everybody* called him Walrus Face. He's been out to get me ever since."

"That's an insult," I said, "to walruses!"

"Hold on," said Andrea. "Dr. Carbles has been out to get you all these years just because you gave him a silly nickname?"

"There's more to it than that," Mr. Klutz told us. "Milton was also jealous of me because he went bald at a very young age and I had a full head of hair."

"YOU HAD A FULL HEAD OF HAIR?!" we all said at the same time.

Mr. Klutz has *no* hair at all. I mean *none*.

"Did you think I was born this way?" Mr. Klutz asked.

Mrs. Klutz brought out a photo album

with pictures of Mr. Klutz as a teenager. He had hair down to his shoulders!

"That's sad that your hair stopped growing," said Emily. It looked like there

Me and milton

were tears in her eyes. What a crybaby!

"Oh, it didn't stop growing," Mr. Klutz told us. "It still grows. Only now it grows out of my ears and nose. I have to trim it every week."

Ew, disgusting! I thought I was gonna throw up.

"Wait a minute," Andrea said. "Dr. Carbles isn't bald."

"Yes he is," said Mr. Klutz. "He wears a toupee. Shhhh! Don't tell him I told you. If people found out he's bald, it would drive him crazy."

Andrea's mother said it was time for us to go. Mr. Klutz thanked us for coming.

Just before we pulled out of the driveway,

Mrs. Klutz came running over to the van.

"He's driving me crazy at home!" she said. "You've *got* to get him back to school!"

Far-out, Man!

The next day it was more of the same at school. No talking. No smiling. No laughing. No fun.

Since it was raining at three o'clock, I thought Dr. Carbles might let us skip the after-school march. But he didn't. When the bell rang, he led us out onto the playground and made us march around in the rain. It was horrible.

"Left! Right! Left! Right!" barked Dr. Carbles. "You kids are a disgrace!"

Finally he let us go home. I walked with Ryan and Michael. We were soaked.

"It's not fair!" Ryan said, as we crossed the street next to the school.

"What's not fair?" somebody asked.

It was Mr. Louie, the school crossing guard. He wears bell-bottom pants and tie-dyed shirts, and he always has his guitar with him. Well, actually it's a stop sign. He wrote the word STOP in big letters on the back of his guitar.

We told Mr. Louie all about Dr. Carbles.

"Bummer, man!" Mr. Louie said. "That dude gives off bad vibes."

"And there's nothing we can do about it," Michael said.

"Sure there is!" Mr. Louie told us. "You should protest! That's what they did back in the Sixties, man. It was far-out! Peace and love were in the air. People changed the world by protesting. You can change your world, too!"

It sounded like a great idea. I invited Mr. Louie over to my house after school so he could teach me and the guys how to protest like they did in the Sixties.

Mr. Louie told us that the way to change the world is to sing songs, chant slogans, and hold up signs. Michael made a sign that said POWER TO THE PEOPLE. Ryan made a sign that said DON'T TRUST ANYONE OVER 12. I made a sign that said CARBLES IS LOSING HIS MARBLES!

While we were working on our signs,

Mr. Louie taught us some protest songs, like "Blowin' in the Wind,"**** and "If I Had a Hammer."

I don't get that hammer song. It's about some guy who wants a hammer. Why doesn't he just go to a hardware store and buy one? Hammers don't cost that much. Instead of singing about hammers, I think we should sing "If I Had a Snowboard" or "If I Had an Xbox." That would make a lot more sense than singing about hammers, if you ask me.

Anyway, when me and the guys got to school the next morning, we were ready to protest. We marched around with our

****That's the one that goes, "The ants are my friends, blowin' in the wind."

signs. We chanted slogans. We sang songs. We were in the middle of "If I Had a Snowboard" when Andrea came over to us.

"What are you dumbheads doing?" she asked.

"We're protesting, man!" I said. "We're gonna change the world!"

"You probably don't even change your underwear, Arlo,"

said Andrea, and she went up the steps to school.

"CARBLES NEVER! KLUTZ FOREVER!" chanted Ryan.

"TWO, FOUR, SIX, EIGHT—WHO DO WE APPRECIATE?" chanted Michael. "KLUTZ! KLUTZ! KLUTZ!"

A bunch of kids gathered around to watch. Some of them joined our protest. A few of the teachers joined in, too. Soon we had a big mob protesting. Everything was going great!

And then, you'll never guess in a million hundred years what came rolling out of the playground.

I'm not going to tell you.

Okay, okay, I'll tell you.

It was a tank!

No, not a fish tank, dumbhead. It was one of those big army tanks. And it was heading our way!

The top of the tank opened up, and Dr. Carbles's head popped out.

"GO TO YOUR CLASSROOMS, NOW!" Dr. Carbles hollered into his bullhorn. "I WILL CRUSH YOUR REBELLION!"

Wow! Where do you think Dr. Carbles got a tank? I guess he rented it. You can rent anything, you know. There's probably a place called Rent-a-Tank.

Dr. Carbles was driving the tank straight at us.

"He wouldn't dare run us over," Michael said.

"GET OUT OF THE WAY!" Dr. Carbles shouted. "OR YOU WILL BE LOCKED IN THE DUNGEON ON THE THIRD FLOOR!"

The tank was getting closer! We didn't know what to say! We didn't know what to do! We had to think fast!

"Run for your lives!" I shouted just as the tank was about to rumble over us.

How to Drive Grown-ups Crazy

Well, that whole protest thing was a dumb idea. Luckily none of us got killed. We'd have to think up another way to get rid of Dr. Carbles.

"Remember how we got rid of Ms. Todd?" Ryan said the next morning while we were putting our backpacks away.

Ms. Todd was a substitute teacher at our school. She tried to murder Miss Daisy and take her job, but we caught her. Ms. Todd was odd.

"Yeah, we drove her crazy," I said.

"Then we have to drive *Dr. Carbles* crazy," said Michael.

If there's one thing I'm good at, it's driving grown-ups crazy. There are lots of ways to do that. One way is to say everything they say right after they say it. That's a good one. Sometimes I ask my parents "Why?" over and over again. It drives them nuts.

But it was Neil the nude kid who had the greatest idea in the history of the world.

"We should steal Dr. Carbles's toupee!" Neil said.

Yeah! Mr. Klutz told us that if anybody ever found out Dr. Carbles was bald, it would drive him crazy! Neil's idea was genius! He should be in the gifted and talented program.

The only problem was, how were we going to steal Dr. Carbles's toupee?

"We could sneak into his house in the middle of the night and rip it off his head," suggested Michael.

"Nah," Ryan said. "He probably has an electric fence and a moat around his house."

"We could rent a giant wind machine and blow it off his head," suggested Michael. "You can rent anything."

"Nah," Ryan said. "It costs a lot of money to rent a giant wind machine."

That's when I got the greatest idea in the history of the world.

"Hey!" I said. "Every day after lunch, Dr. Carbles stands outside and watches us march around the playground, right?"

"Yeah," Michael said. "So what?"

"Well, he has a fishing pole in his office," I told the guys. "We could hang the fishing pole out the second-floor window and go fishing for toupee!"

"You're a genius!" Neil the nude kid

told me.

I should get the No Bell Prize. That's a prize they give out to people who don't have bells.

During lunch me and Neil snuck out of the vomitorium. We slinked around the halls like secret agents. Nobody was around. All the teachers must have been eating in the teachers' lounge.

I opened the door to Dr. Carbles's office. It was empty. Perfect! I grabbed the fishing pole, and we tore out of there.

We ran up the steps to the second floor. I handed Neil the pole and opened a window. We peeked out. Dr. Carbles was right below us, standing there with his bullhorn. The kids were just starting to march out of the vomitorium.

"Left! Right!" Dr. Carbles yelled at the kids. "March, you weasels!"

"This is gonna be great!" Neil giggled as he stuck the fishing pole out the window. "He'll go crazy once we steal his toupee."

"Okay," I told Neil, "drop the hook now."

Neil lowered the line until the hook was hanging right above Dr. Carbles's head.

"A little to the left," I told Neil. "Lower!"

Neil was having a hard time hooking the toupee.

"My arms are getting tired," Neil said.

I grabbed the pole. Neil helped me

guide the hook. It was not easy! The hook kept blowing around.

"Any nibbles yet?" Neil asked.

"Nope." But right after I said that, I felt a little pull on the line. "Hey, I think I got it!"

I started reeling in the toupee, but there was just one problem. It wouldn't come off Dr. Carbles's head! So I pulled harder.

"It's a big one!" I told Neil. "It's a fighter!"

I kept tugging on the fishing pole, but the toupee just wouldn't budge.

"It must be glued on good!" Neil said.

"Maybe they took hair off other parts of his body and planted it on his head," I said. "I saw that on a TV commercial once."

"That's disgusting!" said Neil.

Suddenly Dr. Carbles grabbed his toupee and looked up at us.

"What's the meaning of this!" he shouted.

Uh-oh. I dropped the pole. It fell out the window and almost hit Dr. Carbles on the head.

"A.J., report to my office immediately!" he hollered.

"Oooooooooooooooh!" went all the kids on the playground.

That's it. My life was over. I would have to move to Antarctica and live with the penguins.

The Torture Room

10

When I got to Dr. Carbles's office, he told me to sit in the chair next to his desk. Then he just stared at me. He looked really mad.

"Are you going to be Frank?" I asked.

He didn't say anything. He pulled down the shades to make the room dark.

Then he turned on his desk lamp and pointed the light on me.

"Who told you I wear a toupee, A.J.?" asked Dr. Carbles. "Huh? Who told you?"

I was pretty sure I had the right to remain silent. I saw that on a TV show once.

Besides, I was too scared to say anything.

"The teachers are plotting against me, aren't they?" Dr. Carbles said. "I don't trust them. I see the way they look at me. They hate me. Everybody hates me."

I kept my mouth shut. If you don't say anything, you can't say anything dumb.

"Did Mr. Docker tell you about my toupee?" asked Dr. Carbles. "Or was it Miss Lazar? You can tell me, A.J."

His face was right next to mine. His breath smelled like rotten eggs. I was shaking. I thought I was gonna die.

"Cat got your tongue, eh?" Dr. Carbles asked. "Well, I have ways to make you talk."

Oh no! He was going to torture me!

"Here, I want you to read this," said Dr. Carbles.

"What is it?" I asked.

"A book."

"A *book*?!" I exclaimed. "With words?"

"That's right," Dr. Carbles said. "Read it."

"Reading is boring," I told him.

"READ IT!" he shouted. "Every word! Cover to cover! Let's go. I don't have all day."

Sweat was rolling down my face.

"No! No!" I cried. "Not reading! Anything but that! Okay, I'll talk! I'll talk!"

"Smart boy," Dr. Carbles said, taking the book away. "I knew you'd see it my way."

"It was Mr. Klutz," I admitted. "I went

over to his house. He told me about your toupee. He told me about the skateboarding team. He told me he called you Walrus Face. He told me *everything*."

"Klutz, eh?" sneered Dr. Carbles. "Klutz told you that? Oh, I'm going to get him. I'm going to get him good. *Nobody* calls me Walrus Face and gets away with it!"

"Please don't tell Mr. Klutz I told you. I promised him I wouldn't tell. Please, Frank?"

"Get out of here!" Dr. Carbles hollered. "And stop calling me Frank or I'll get the summer reading list!"

I ran out of his office as fast as I could.

The Big Skate-off

11

When I got to school the next morning, I could hear the sound of hammering. It was coming from the gym. That was weird. I went over to the gym and opened the door. You'll never believe in a million hundred years what I saw.

Five guys in overalls were building a half-pipe! Right there in the gym!

Wow! We were going to go skateboarding in fizz ed!

The fizz ed teacher, Miss Small, is off the wall. She usually has us juggle scarves and balance feathers on our fingers. But we were finally going to do something cool! We were going to skateboard! It was the greatest day of my life.

Me and the guys were so excited, we could hardly stand it.

"When do we go to fizz ed?" we kept asking Miss Daisy.

"I don't know," said Miss Daisy, who doesn't know anything.

Finally, at the end of the day, Mrs. Patty made an announcement over the loudspeaker. She said that everybody had to report to the gym.

"Hooray!" all the boys yelled. Miss Daisy had to keep telling us to stop running the whole way there.

When we got there, the half-pipe was finished, and Dr. Carbles was standing in front of it. He was holding a skateboard.

"Where's Miss Small?" I asked. "Are we going to skateboard in fizz ed?"

"No!" shouted Dr. Carbles. "This half-pipe isn't for you. It's for *me.*"

"Boooooo!" yelled all the boys.

We were really mad as we sat down on the bleachers. But we didn't stay mad for long, because you'll never believe who walked into the door at the other end of the gym.

Nobody. If you walked into a door, it would hurt. But guess who walked into the door*way*?

It was Mr. Klutz! And he was holding a skateboard. Everybody cheered.

"Hooray for Mr. Klutz!" we all shouted.

Dr. Carbles and Mr. Klutz stood facing each other at opposite sides of the gym. They looked like two gunslingers on one of those old Western TV shows, except they had skateboards instead of guns. Everybody got quiet. You could hear a pin drop.

"So, we meet again, Klutz," said Dr. Carbles. "I thought you'd be too chicken to show up."

"I will outskate you *any*time," Mr. Klutz said. "You're going down, Walrus Face!"

"Oh, snap!" Ryan whispered.

"Mr. Klutz is gonna blow the doors off Dr. Carbles!" I told the guys.

Mr. Klutz and Dr. Carbles climbed up to the top of the half-pipe. Dr. Carbles picked up his bullhorn.

"Finally, all the world will know who the best skateboarder is!" he hollered. "Ha-ha-ha! Revenge will be sweet!"

We all started chanting: "TWO, FOUR, SIX, EIGHT—WHO DO WE APPRECIATE? KLUTZ! KLUTZ! KLUTZ!"

Dr. Carbles and Mr. Klutz dropped into the half-pipe at the same time. Dr. Carbles did a vert bomb drop. Mr. Klutz did a combination inward heelflip/outside boardslide. Dr. Carbles did a polejam. Mr. Klutz did a boomerang.

It was awesome! Everybody in the gym was yelling and screaming their heads off. Even the teachers!

Then, just as Dr. Carbles was doing a

monkeyflip jawbreaker, Mr. Klutz did a stalefish McTwist. They crashed into each other in midair! Dr. Carbles's toupee went

flying off his head! The two of them landed together in a tangle of arms and legs. It was a real Kodak moment. And we got to see it live and in person.

"Oh, my leg!" moaned Dr. Carbles.

"Ouch! My head!" moaned Mr. Klutz.

The two of them were lying at the bottom of the half-pipe, freaking out. Mrs. Cooney, the beautiful school nurse, came running over with a first-aid kit. And you'll never believe in a million hundred years who walked in the gym at that exact moment.

I'm not going to tell you.

Okay, okay, I'll tell you.

It was Mrs. Haney, the superintendent

of all the schools in the county!

"Carbles!" she shouted. "What's the meaning of this?"

Dr. Carbles looked at Mr. Klutz. Mr. Klutz looked at Mrs. Haney. Mrs. Haney looked at Dr. Carbles. Everybody was looking at each other.

"It's a half-pipe, ma'am," Dr. Carbles said. "I challenged Klutz to a little competition."

"You were hired to bring order and discipline to this school!" Mrs. Haney yelled. "I didn't bring you here so you could build a half-poop and ride a skateboard!"

"B-b-but . . . ," said Dr. Carbles.

"Carbles!" shouted Mrs. Haney. "You're FIRED!"

Dr. Carbles limped out of the gym, sobbing. What a crybaby!

You Can Rent Anything

"Watch out!" somebody screamed.

It was the day before Thanksgiving. Some crazy lunatic dressed like a Pilgrim was tearing down the sidewalk on a skateboard. He must have built up too much speed. The guy was weaving around kids, totally out of control.

"Run for your lives!" somebody shouted.

The skateboard must have hit a crack in the sidewalk, because the next thing anybody knew, the Pilgrim went flying through the air like a superhero. Kids were diving out of the way. Dogs were running as fast as they could.

The skateboarding Pilgrim crash-landed in the bushes in front of the school. You'll never believe in a million hundred years who it was.

It was Mr. Klutz!

"Good morning, Mr. Klutz," said Mrs. Cooney as she walked past.

"Good morning, Mrs. Cooney," he replied. "Beautiful day, isn't it?"

"Lovely."

Mr. Klutz got up, brushed himself off, and walked up the front steps, like it was totally normal to skateboard to school dressed as a Pilgrim and crash headfirst into the bushes.

Everybody clapped and cheered when

we realized Mr. Klutz had been hired to be our principal again. No more marching. No more uniforms. No more Dr. Carbles. It was the best day in the history of the world.

In the afternoon we were called down to the all-purpose room for an assembly. Mr. Klutz went up on the stage, and everybody gave him a standing ovation.

"Well, I have good news and bad news," Mr. Klutz told us. "The bad news is that even though you all made beautiful Thanksgiving displays, I can't marry a turkey like I promised."

"What happened to Gobbles?" Emily asked.

"I'm having her for dinner tomorrow," Mr. Klutz said.

"What's the good news?" I shouted.

"You'll see." Mr. Klutz went behind the curtain. You'll never believe in a million hundred years what he brought out with him.

A live pig!

"I'm going to marry this pig instead," he told us.

Everybody started cheering and stamping their feet.

"Where did you get a pig?" yelled Ryan.

"From Rent-a-Pig," Mr. Klutz said. "You can rent anything, you know."

Mrs. Roopy came out onstage with a

book. She was wearing a man's suit and tie.

"It's Mrs. Roopy!" everybody yelled.

"I'm not Mrs. Roopy," said Mrs. Roopy. "I'm the justice of the peace. Mr. Klutz, do you take this pig to be your wife—to love, honor, and cherish till death do you part?"

"I do," said Mr. Klutz.

"Pig, do you take Mr. Klutz to be your husband—in sickness and in health, till death do you part?"

"Oink," said the pig.

"This is so romantic!" Andrea whispered.

"I now pronounce you man and wife," said Mrs. Roopy. "Mr. Klutz, you may kiss the pig."

Mr. Klutz bent down and kissed the

pig, right on the lips! Ew, disgusting! That was the second time I saw Mr. Klutz kiss a pig. He must really love pigs.

After the assembly we went back to

Miss Daisy's class to get ready for dismissal. She wished us a Happy Thanksgiving and made us go around in a circle to say what we were thankful for.

"I'm thankful that Mr. Klutz is back," said Andrea.

"I'm thankful that Dr. Carbles is gone," said Michael.

The three-o'clock bell rang.

"What are you thankful for, A.J.?" asked Miss Daisy.

"I'm thankful that we don't have school for four more days," I said. Then I ran out of there.

Maybe Dr. Carbles will take a chill pill

and get his job back. Maybe we'll be allowed to keep the half-pipe and go skateboarding in fizz ed. Maybe Mr. Klutz and the pig will go on a honeymoon and live happily ever after. Maybe Mr. and Mrs. Klutz will get divorced because Mr. Klutz is always kissing pigs and marrying them. Maybe hair will stop growing out of Mr. Klutz's nose and back on the top of his head, where it belongs. Maybe my weird school will become more like a normal school.

But it won't be easy!